This book belongs to

_____

Walt Disney's
Sleeping Beauty

A READ-ALOUD STORYBOOK

Adapted by Catherine Hapka
Illustrated by the Disney Storybook Artists
at Global Art Development

Random House 🏠 New York

Copyright © 1986, 1993, 1996, 2003 Disney Enterprises, Inc. All rights reserved under International and Pan-American Copyright Conventions. Published in the United States by Random House, Inc., New York, and simultaneously in Canada by Random House of Canada Limited, Toronto, in conjunction with Disney Enterprises, Inc. RANDOM HOUSE and colophon are registered trademarks of Random House, Inc. Originally published in different form by Disney Press in 1986, 1993, and 1996. Library of Congress Control Number: 2002102657   ISBN: 0-7364-2098-3
Printed in the United States of America
10 9 8 7 6 5 4 3 2 1
First Edition

www.randomhouse.com/kids/disney

A Princess Is Born

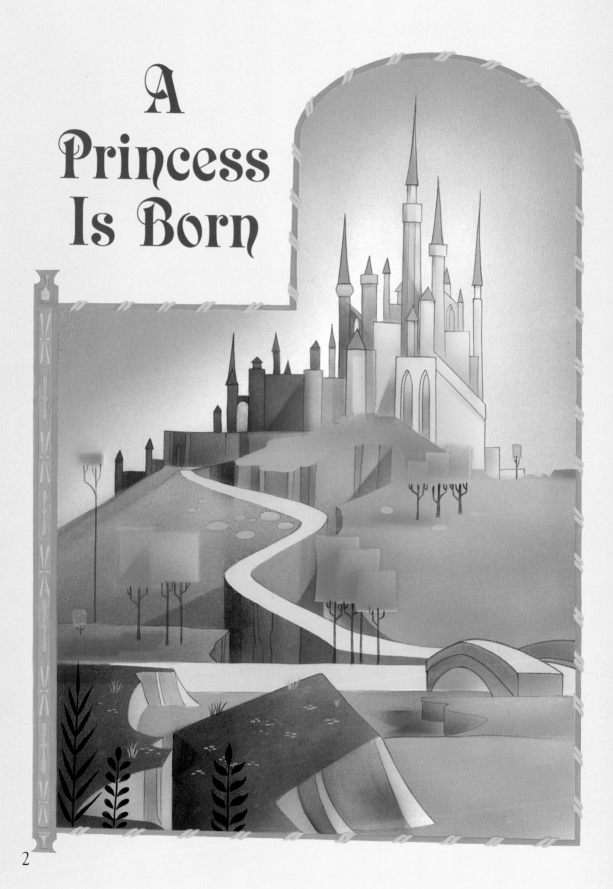

Once upon a time, there lived a kind king and gentle queen who wanted to have a child. After many years, they had a baby girl. They named the baby Aurora.

The king and queen were so happy that they held a celebration. Visitors came from all over the land, including King Hubert, who ruled a nearby kingdom, and his young son, Prince Phillip. The two kings decided that Phillip and Aurora would marry one day and unite the kingdoms.

Soon the celebration began, and three good fairies, Flora, Fauna, and Merryweather, floated into the room. They had come to give special magical gifts to the baby princess. Flora said, "My gift shall be the gift of beauty." Fauna said, "My gift shall be the gift of song."

But before Merryweather could give her gift to the baby, a gust of wind blew open the doors. There was a flash of lightning, a crack of thunder, and then darkness. A bright flame appeared in the middle of the hall. It slowly took the shape of the wicked fairy Maleficent!

Maleficent was so angry about not being invited to the celebration that she put a curse on the baby.

"Before the sun sets on her sixteenth birthday," she said, "she shall prick her finger on the spindle of a spinning wheel . . . and die."

"Oh, no!" the queen cried.

"Seize that creature!" King Stefan, Aurora's father, ordered. But before the guards could reach Maleficent, she disappeared in a burst of fire and smoke.

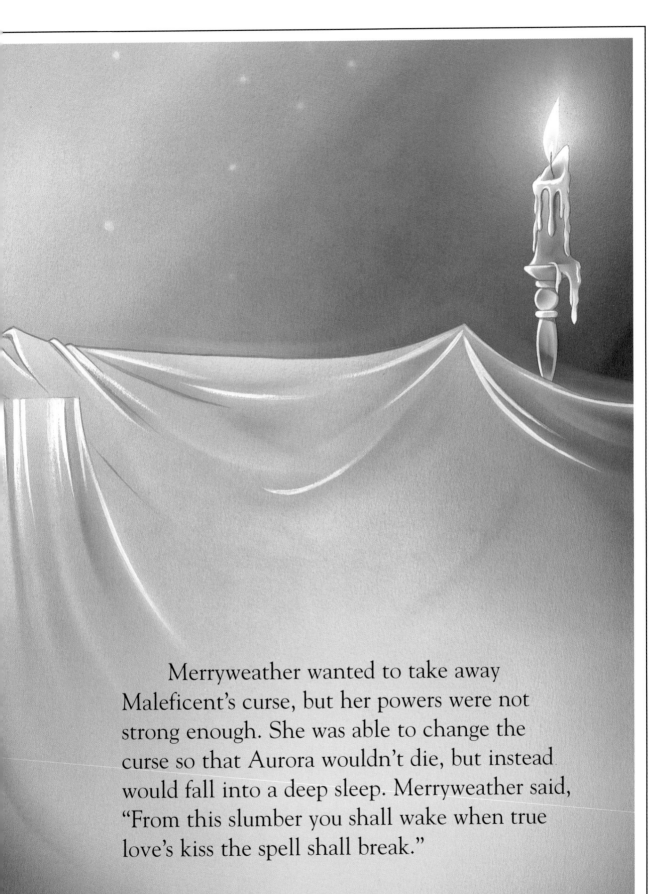

Merryweather wanted to take away
Maleficent's curse, but her powers were not
strong enough. She was able to change the
curse so that Aurora wouldn't die, but instead
would fall into a deep sleep. Merryweather said,
"From this slumber you shall wake when true
love's kiss the spell shall break."

King Stefan was so worried about Maleficent's curse that he had every spinning wheel in the kingdom burned. But Flora came up with a better plan to protect the princess. The three fairies would transform themselves into peasants and raise her deep in the forest. In this disguise, they would use no magic, so that Maleficent would not be able to find them. Once the curse ended, they would return Aurora to the palace.

The king and queen wanted to do everything they could to protect Aurora, so they agreed to Flora's plan. One night soon after, the fairies slipped away with the baby princess.

Briar Rose

Many years passed, and high on the Forbidden Mountain, Maleficent had lost her patience. It was almost Aurora's sixteenth birthday, and her evil helpers still hadn't found the princess.

"Sixteen years and not a trace of her!" Maleficent shouted. "Are you sure you've searched everywhere?"

19

Maleficent's last hope of finding the princess was her raven. She ordered the black bird to circle far and wide until it found a sixteen-year-old maiden with beautiful gold hair and rose-red lips.

Meanwhile, Princess Aurora had grown up to be sweet and lovely. The fairies called her Briar Rose and loved her like a daughter. On her sixteenth birthday, they sent her into the forest to pick berries and play with the animals so that they would have enough time to prepare for her party without using magic.

Briar Rose wandered along, singing a song to her
animal friends about the true love she wished for.
Nearby, a young prince heard Briar Rose's sweet singing.
He asked his horse, Samson, to take him to her.

Samson started galloping toward Briar Rose, but when he jumped over a log, his master fell into a creek. "No carrots for you!" scolded the prince. He got up out of the water and laid his hat, cape, and boots out to dry.

When the prince wasn't looking, some of the animals borrowed his things. They dressed up for Briar Rose, pretending to be the prince of her dreams.

The prince approached Briar Rose and began to sing along with her. Soon they started dancing together and fell deeply in love.

But when the prince asked
her name, Briar Rose remembered
that she wasn't allowed to speak
to strangers. Even so, before she
left, she invited the prince to
come to the cottage that night.

Back at the cottage, the fairies were having trouble preparing for Briar Rose's birthday party. Fauna's cake leaned all the way to one side, and the dress Flora was making didn't look right, either. The fairies had given up using magic, but now they were desperate, so they went to the attic to find something to help them.

Sure that no one would see them, the fairies made everything perfect—with a little help from their magic wands.

But while Flora and Merryweather were
arguing about the color of Briar Rose's dress,
they accidentally let their magic escape up
the chimney.

Just as Maleficent's raven was flying overhead searching for Aurora, colorful sparkles from the magic wands shot out of the cottage's chimney. The raven quickly flew back to the Forbidden Mountain to tell Maleficent that it had found the good fairies—and the princess!

When Briar Rose returned home, she told the fairies all about the handsome stranger she'd met. The fairies knew that it was time to tell Aurora the truth.

They explained to Aurora that she was a princess
and was promised to marry Prince Phillip. Aurora
cried and cried because she thought this meant she
couldn't marry the young man she had met in the
forest. Little did she know the young man was
Phillip! The fairies set off to return the princess to
her home and to her parents, the king and queen.

The Magic Spell

When they reached the palace, the fairies left Aurora alone while they went to find her parents. Suddenly a strange glow appeared in front of the princess. In a trance, she followed the light up a winding staircase.

The long staircase led to a hidden room with a spinning wheel in it. When Aurora stepped inside, Maleficent appeared and said, "Touch the spindle—touch it, I say!" Powerless against the evil fairy's magic, the princess obeyed and pricked her finger on the spindle's sharp point.

The good fairies returned to the hall and
found Aurora gone, so they followed the
stairway to the hidden room. There they found
evil Maleficent standing over the fallen princess.

Merryweather, Fauna, and Flora were very worried that the king and queen would find Aurora in her deep sleep. They decided to put everyone else at the palace into a deep sleep as well until they could undo Maleficent's curse.

King Hubert was visiting the palace that night. As he was falling asleep, Flora heard him say that Prince Phillip wanted to marry a peasant girl. "Briar Rose!" Flora cried. Prince Phillip was arriving at the cottage that very moment! She quickly found the other fairies, and they rushed to meet him.

48

A Daring Prince

But when the prince entered the cottage, Maleficent and her evil creatures were waiting there, ready to trap him. She knew that the brave prince was the only person who could undo her curse on Aurora, so Maleficent had to keep him away from the princess.

Maleficent took the prince back to her castle and locked him in her dungeon. She revealed to him that the peasant girl was Princess Aurora and that only his kiss could awaken her. Phillip knew he had to escape to save his true love.

Just then, the good fairies appeared.
They freed Prince Phillip and gave him
the magical Shield of Virtue and Sword
of Truth. "These weapons of righteousness
will triumph over evil," they told him.

As the good fairies and Phillip were leaving the dungeon, Maleficent's raven spotted them. The bla[ck] bird quickly told its wicked mistress that the prince had escaped.

Maleficent would do anything to keep the prince away from Aurora. She put a wall of thorns around him. Using the Sword of Truth, Phillip quickly cut a path through the branches and rode away on Samson.

As the prince approached the castle's bridge, Maleficent turned herself into a terrible dragon and blasted him with red-hot flames. Phillip used his shield to protect himself and Samson.

The good fairies saw that Prince Phillip was in danger, so they sprinkled his sword with fairy dust. "Now, Sword of Truth, fly swift and sure, that evil die and good endure," they said. The prince threw his sword at the dragon with all his might. The beast fell back and plunged over the edge of the cliff!

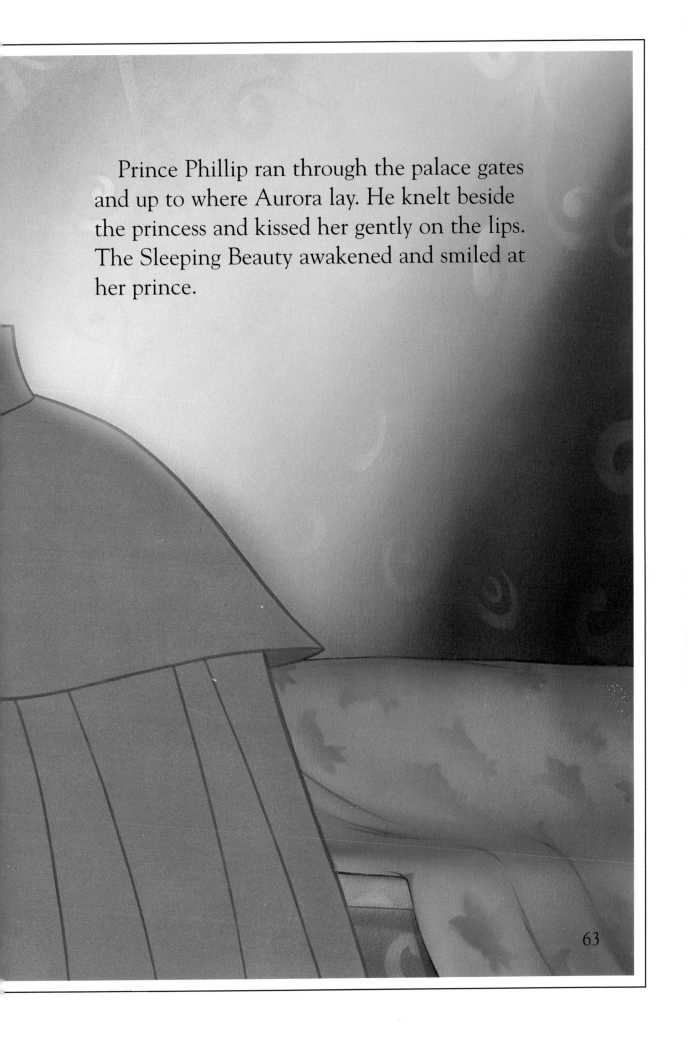

Prince Phillip ran through the palace gates
and up to where Aurora lay. He knelt beside
the princess and kissed her gently on the lips.
The Sleeping Beauty awakened and smiled at
her prince.

Before long, everyone else in the kingdom awoke, including King Stefan and the queen. The princess and her parents hugged joyfully, happy to be reunited at last. Soon after, Princess Aurora married Prince Phillip . . . and they lived happily ever after.